The World According

to Mister Rogers

The World According to Mister Rogers

to Mister Rogers

Important Things to Remember

FRED ROGERS

hachette
BOOKS

NEW YORK   BOSTON

Hachette Books
Hachette Book Group
1290 Avenue of the Americas, New York, NY 10104
hachettebooks.com
twitter.com/hachettebooks

Originally published in hardcover and ebook by Hyperion in 2003.
Reissued: May 2019

Hachette Books is an imprint of Perseus Books, LLC, a subsidiary of Hachette Book Group, Inc. The Hachette Books name and logo are trademarks of Hachette Book Group, Inc.

The publisher is not responsible for websites (or their content) that are not owned by the publisher.

LCCN: 2003056634
ISBN: 978-0-316-49271-3 (hardcover)

Printed in the United States of America

LSC-C

Printing 9, 2021

THIS BOOK IS DEDICATED,
IN FRED ROGERS' MEMORY,
TO ANYONE WHO HAS
LOVED YOU INTO BEING.

CONTENTS

Joanne Rogers

He has achieved success who has lived well, laughed often, and loved much, who has enjoyed the trust of pure women, the respect of intelligent men, and the love of little children, who has filled his niche and accomplished his task, who has left the world better than he found it, whether by an improved poppy, a perfect poem, or a rescued soul, who has never lacked appreciation of Earth's beauty or failed to express it, who has always looked for the best in others and given them the best he had, whose life was an inspiration, whose memory a benediction.

—Bessie Anderson Stanley

There were always quotes like that tucked away in Fred's wallet, next to his neatly folded bills, or in the pages of his daily planner book. Perhaps he liked having words of wisdom close to him, as if he wanted—or needed—to be constantly reminded of what was important in life. The outside world may have thought his qualities of wisdom and strength came naturally to him, but those close to him knew that he was constantly striving to be the best that he could be. He was as human as the rest of us.

I first met Fred at Rollins College. He was planning to transfer there from Dartmouth College—to major in music—and a group of us music students were asked to show him around. We were delighted at the prospect of a "new kid" on campus. One of our friends had a wonderful, roomy old (almost antique!) Franklin car, and we all went to the train station to welcome Fred. After the tour, we took him to see the music rooms, where we spent many hours of our college lives, and he immediately sat down at a piano. We loved his playing. Few of our small group could play the jazz and popular songs of our day with so much ease and grace. And he could play the classics, too. This "new kid" really had talent!

The next semester he arrived, and he "fit in" beautifully. He was a lot of fun and became quite popular, and after a year or so he fulfilled the leadership potential that would follow him the rest of his life. We both formed lasting friendships at Rollins. Fred and I were together much of the time and our friendship became deep and strong. I suppose our friends probably thought of us as "a couple." We went to many dances together, and once Fred and I won first prize for our Raggedy Ann and Andy costumes. The prize was a big bottle of champagne—what a gift for two teetotalers! We had great fun going from table to table and pouring it for everyone else.

It was not *all* fun and games for Fred—he had his struggles, too, as we all did. I remember his moaning and groaning to us, "I just *know* I'm going to fail this course!" Of course, we'd all get worried for him. Then he'd get an A— and we'd all get mad at him. (When he graduated, it was with a double major and high honors.) But Fred worked with discipline, while being a good friend to many during those happy college years.

Later on, he brought that same sense of hard work and inner discipline to his work. Whether he was working on a script for the *Neighborhood* programs or on a speech, he fretted over the words, attempting to make the content meaningful. I can remember his saying over and over again, as he worked at the fourth or fifth draft of whatever he happened to be writing, "Simple is better."

Since Fred had lost a year by transferring from one college to another, I was in the class ahead of him and went on to Florida State University for a master's degree in music, where I remained for the next two years. There was a trip back to Rollins to see Fred graduate, and we wrote letters to each other occasionally. I was busy and he was busy. He was, by then, in New York at NBC, in an apprentice program, and fortunately his assignments were with the music programs, among them the *NBC Opera Theatre*. How stimulating and challenging those days of early television were for Fred. By the spring of his first year there, April 1952, I got a letter from him with a proposal of marriage! I was too excited to take the time to write a letter, so I accepted his proposal from a pay-phone booth. We were married in July 1952.

After seven years of marriage, our first son was born, and just twenty-one months later we welcomed our second son into our family. Fred was, by that time, very busy with his early work in Pittsburgh, developing an educational television program for children and attending classes at the theological seminary (during his lunch hour or in the evenings). His early work in TV was all behind-the-scenes, as puppeteer and musician, and that was quite comfortable for him, because Fred was basically shy. It took courage and a lot of support when he faced the cameras for the first *Neighborhood* programs. Someone once asked which one of his puppets resembled him the most. It was, of course, Daniel Striped Tiger—an uncharacteristically shy tiger. Despite Fred's tendency to shyness, that trait never got in the way of his capacity to make many friends, to whom he readily lent an empathetic ear. Fred was always a good listener for as long as I knew him.

He was most relaxed at the piano. Often he'd play his own music that he'd written for the *Neighborhood* programs. Sometimes he'd improvise music that would be very complex and emotional in tone. It was his way of dealing with his feelings. Then sometimes he'd just enjoy playing a lot of different tunes that he loved. Some were songs, like "Misty," that Johnny Costa (the inimitable music director/pianist for the *Neighborhood*) had arranged for Fred. What a treat it was for those of us who were able to listen—from a distance, so as not to disturb his piano reverie.

What influenced and changed his life more than anything, in my opinion, was what he learned from Dr. Margaret McFarland. She was his mentor in the child development graduate program at the University of Pittsburgh. She let him know it was okay to be sensitive, and helped him find the courage to be himself with children—and with the rest of the world.

Margaret once said that Fred was more in touch with his own childhood than anyone she knew. Under her guidance, he brought his puppets and music to children, and she helped him learn about child development. But I also saw the strength she gave him by supporting him to bring his own creative self to what he was learning. I've always thought of Fred as a creative artist, and I truly believe it was through Margaret that he was able to find the courage and determination to use his knowledge and talents—and in fact, his whole life—in the service of children.

The person Fred became in his later years came out of growth and struggle. As he got older, it seemed as if the nurturing of his soul and mind became more and more important. He read with pleasure the works of friends and others he admired and respected, and he began each day with prayers for a legion of family and friends and, in general, for the peacemakers of the world. Reading the Bible was also part of this early morning routine—before he went for his daily swim. He worked hard at being the best he could be. In fact, it seems to me he worked a lot more than he played. Discipline was his very strong suit. If I were asked for three words to describe him, I think those words would be *courage, love,* and *discipline*—perhaps in that very order.

He worked so hard at being other-oriented (not self-centered) that he'd often express himself by using the first person plural. He'd say, "*We're* doing this or that." It was almost always "*we.*" People might sometimes have wondered who else he was including. Perhaps he was simply making an effort to ensure that his colleagues and coworkers were equally recognized and valued for the work in which they all were so invested. That would've been Fred's wish.

A quote he loved especially—and carried around with him—was from Mary Lou Kownacki: "There isn't anyone you couldn't love once you've heard their story." There were many times I wanted to be angry at someone, and Fred would say, "But I wonder what was going on in that person's day." His capacity for understanding always amazed me.

When we were together, he was able to show his lighter side—perhaps I even enabled it sometimes, as did several of his friends who had "the gift of whimsy." He could laugh heartily and with much pleasure at pure silliness, and was, at times, the funniest person I have known. He was well aware, also, how much I love to laugh, and that was a way he could please me. That sense of humor survived up to his last days. After fifty years of marriage (celebrated in July 2002), we had collected a million laughs—just two or three words could send us off into gales of merriment.

When I think of the entire *persona* of Fred Rogers, my inclination is to put him on a very high pedestal, despite the frailties that are part of being human. Oh, did I mention what a *kind* person he was? I suppose that is part of everyone's experience of Fred—even those who knew him for only a couple of minutes. I don't mean to sound boastful, but he was my icon before he was anyone else's. Being Mrs. Fred Rogers has been the most remarkable life I could ever have imagined.

The
Courage
to Be
Yourself

Discovering the truth about ourselves is a lifetime's work, but it's worth the effort.

Some days, doing "the best we can" may still fall short of what we would like to be able to do, but life isn't perfect—on any front—and doing what we can with what we have is the most we should expect of ourselves or anyone else.

Confronting our feelings and giving them appropriate expression always takes strength, not weakness. It takes strength to acknowledge our anger, and sometimes more strength yet to curb the aggressive urges anger may bring and to channel them into nonviolent outlets. It takes strength to face our sadness and to grieve and to let our grief and our anger flow in tears when they need to. It takes strength to talk about our feelings and to reach out for help and comfort when we need it.

The Truth Will Make Me Free

What if I were very, very sad
And all I did was smile?
I wonder after awhile
What might become of my sadness?

What if I were very, very angry
And all I did was sit
And never think about it?
What might become of my anger?

Where would they go,
And what would they do,
If I couldn't let them out?

Maybe I'd fall, maybe get sick
Or doubt.

But what if I could know the truth
And say just how I feel?
I think I'd learn a lot that's real
About freedom.

Music is the one art we all have inside.
We may not be able to play an instrument,
but we can sing along or clap or tap our
feet. Have you ever seen a baby bouncing
up and down in the crib in time to some
music? When you think of it, some of that
baby's first messages from his or her parents
may have been lullabies, or at least the
music of their speaking voices. All of us have
had the experience of hearing a tune from
childhood and having that melody evoke a
memory or a feeling. The music we hear
early on tends to stay with us all our lives.

Who you are inside is what helps you make and do everything in life.

There's no "should" or "should not" when
it comes to having feelings. They're part of
who we are and their origins are beyond
our control. When we can believe that,
we may find it easier to make constructive
choices about what to do with those
feelings.

Whatever we choose to imagine can be as private as we want it to be. Nobody knows what you're thinking or feeling unless you share it.

How many times have you noticed that it's the little quiet moments in the midst of life that seem to give the rest extra-special meaning?

There's a nurturing element to all human beings, whenever they themselves have been nurtured, and it's going to be expressed one way or another.

When my mother or my grandmother tried to keep me from climbing too high, my grandfather would say, "Let the kid walk on the wall. He's got to learn to do things for himself." I loved my grandfather for trusting me so much. His name was Fred McFeely. No wonder I included a lively, elderly delivery man in our television "neighborhood" whom we named "Mr. McFeely."

Part of the problem with the word *disabilities* is that it immediately suggests an inability to see or hear or walk or do other things that many of us take for granted. But what of people who can't feel? Or talk about their feelings? Or manage their feelings in constructive ways? What of people who aren't able to form close and strong relationships? And people who cannot find fulfillment in their lives, or those who have lost hope, who live in disappointment and bitterness and find in life no joy, no love? These, it seems to me, are the real disabilities.

It's not the honors and the prizes and the fancy outsides of life that ultimately nourish our souls. It's the knowing that we can be trusted, that we never have to fear the truth, that the bedrock of our very being is firm.

All our lives, we rework the things from our childhood, like feeling good about ourselves, managing our angry feelings, being able to say good-bye to people we love.

In order to express our sense of reality, we must use some kind of symbol: words or notes or shades of paint or television pictures or sculpted forms. None of those symbols or images can ever completely satisfy us because they can never be any more than what they are—a fragment of a reflection of what we feel reality to be.

I remember after my grandfather's death, seeing Dad in the hall with tears streaming down his face. I don't think I had ever seen him cry before. I'm glad I did see him. It helped me know that it was okay for men to cry. Many years later, when my father himself died, I cried; and way down deep I knew he would have said it was all right.

It isn't only famous movie stars who want to be alone. Whenever I hear someone speak of privacy, I find myself thinking once again how real and deep the need for such times is for all human beings . . . at all ages.

Solitude is different from loneliness, and it doesn't have to be a lonely kind of thing.

You rarely have time for everything you want in this life, so you need to make choices. And hopefully your choices can come from a deep sense of who you are.

Most of us, I believe, admire strength.
It's something we tend to respect in others,
desire for ourselves, and wish for our
children. Sometimes, though, I wonder if
we confuse strength with other words—
like *aggression* and even *violence*.
Real strength is neither male nor female;
but it is, quite simply, one of the finest
characteristics that any human being
can possess.

All life events are formative. All contribute to what we become, year by year, as we go on growing. As my friend the poet Kenneth Koch once said, "You aren't just the age you are. You are all the ages you ever have been!"

The values we care about the deepest, and the movements within society that support those values, command our love. When those things that we care about so deeply become endangered, we become enraged. And what a healthy thing that is! Without it, we would never stand up and speak out for what we believe.

I've often hesitated in beginning a project because I've thought, "It'll never turn out to be even remotely like the good idea I have as I start." I could just "feel" how good it *could* be. But I decided that, for the present, I would create the best way I know how and accept the ambiguities.

When I think of Robert Frost's poems, like "The Road Not Taken," I feel the support of someone who is on my side, who understands what life's choices are like, someone who says, "I've been there, and it's okay to go on."

I believe it's a fact of life that what we have is less important than what we make out of what we have. The same holds true for families: It's not how many people there are in a family that counts, but rather the feelings among the people who are there.

I'm proud of you for the times you came in second, or third, or fourth, but what you did was the best you had ever done.

Often when you think you're at the end of something, you're at the beginning of something else. I've felt that many times. My hope for all of us is that "the miles we go before we sleep" will be filled with all the feelings that come from deep caring—delight, sadness, joy, wisdom—and that in all the endings of our life, we will be able to see the new beginnings.

When I was a boy I used to think that *strong* meant having big muscles, great physical power; but the longer I live, the more I realize that real strength has much more to do with what is *not* seen. Real strength has to do with helping others.

The thing I remember best about successful people I've met all through the years is their obvious delight in what they're doing . . . and it seems to have very little to do with worldly success. They just love what they're doing, and they love it in front of others.

I must be an emotional archaeologist because I keep looking for the roots of things, particularly the roots of behavior and why I feel certain ways about certain things.

The Clown in Me

Sometimes I feel when I'm afraid
That I will never make the grade
So I pretend I'm someone else
And show the world my other self.
I'm not quite sure of me, you see
When I have to make a clown of me.

A clown, a clown
I think I'll be a clown.
I think I'll make the people laugh
And laugh all over town. A clown,
That's what I'll be, a clown.

Sometimes I feel all good inside
And haven't got a thing to hide.
My friends all tell me I'm the best;
They think I'm better than the rest.
It's times like this I act myself
And I let the clown stay on the shelf.

Myself, myself
I think I'll be myself.
I think I'll let the people see
The comfortable inside of me.
Myself, I'll be myself.

It's only when I feel let down
I might be scared into a clown.
But, he can be himself
When I can be myself, myself.
I think I'll be myself.

Little by little we human beings are
confronted with situations that give us
more and more clues that we aren't perfect.

The child is in me still . . . and sometimes not so still.

Understanding

Love

Understanding love is one of the hardest
things in the world.

Deep within us—no matter who we are—
there lives a feeling of wanting to be
lovable, of wanting to be the kind of person
that others like to be with. And the greatest
thing we can do is to let people know that
they are loved and capable of loving.

Love isn't a state of perfect caring. It is an active noun like *struggle*. To love someone is to strive to accept that person exactly the way he or she is, right here and now.

Each generation, in its turn, is a link between all that has gone before and all that comes after. That is true genetically, and it is equally true in the transmission of identity. Our parents gave us what they were able to give, and we took what we could of it and made it part of ourselves. If we knew our grandparents, and even great-grandparents, we will have taken from them what they could offer us, too. All that helped to make us who we are. We, in our turn, will offer what we can of ourselves to our children and their offspring.

It's the people we love the most who can make us feel the gladdest . . . and the maddest! Love and anger are such a puzzle! It's hard for us, as adults, to understand and manage our angry feelings toward parents, spouses, and children, or to keep their anger toward us in perspective. It's a different kind of anger from the kind we may feel toward strangers because it is so deeply intertwined with caring and attachment.

If the day ever came when we were able to accept ourselves and our children exactly as we and they are, then, I believe, we would have come very close to an ultimate understanding of what "good" parenting means. It's part of being human to fall short of that total acceptance—and often far short. But one of the most important gifts a parent can give a child is the gift of accepting that child's uniqueness.

It always helps to have people we love beside us when we have to do difficult things in life.

People have said, "Don't cry" to other people for years and years, and all it has ever meant is, "I'm too uncomfortable when you show your feelings. Don't cry." I'd rather have them say, "Go ahead and cry. I'm here to be with you."

Grandparents are both our past and our future. In some ways they are what has gone before, and in others they are what we will become.

Forgiving and forgetting are often paired together, but the one certainly doesn't necessarily follow the other. Some injuries, real or imagined, we may never be able to forget, even though we say we've forgiven them. Other injuries we may never even be able to say that we forgive. Those are the ones, it seems to me, most likely to involve people we've loved, and so I'm inclined to look at what our experiences of forgiveness may have been like from the first people who loved *us*.

The first time we required forgiveness, we probably did something we shouldn't have when our closest grown-ups thought we should have known better. We made someone angry. We were to blame. What did the first brush with blame begin to teach us?

If we were fortunate, we began to learn that "to err is human." Even good people sometimes do bad things. Errors might mean corrections, apologies, repairs, but they didn't mean that we, as a person, were a bad person in the sight of those we loved. The second thing we learned (if we were fortunate) was that having someone we loved get mad at us did not mean that person had stopped loving us; we had their *unconditional* love, and that meant we would have their forgiveness, too.

One of my wise teachers, Dr. William F. Orr, told me, "There is only one thing evil cannot stand and that is forgiveness."

Love and trust, in the space between what's said and what's heard in our life, can make all the difference in this world.

Competition. It's a word that makes many of us very edgy, and it's a situation that we have probably been living with since we were very small.

For some people competition is a thrill, a stimulation, a challenge. For others, it's a source of sadness and anger and apprehension. For still others, it's a mixture of all those things.

It's not possible to go through life without competing. As one woman told me, "Competition is a part of our everyday life, whether we're competing for a job, or on the soccer field, or for love."

There are many kinds of competition, to be sure. But I think that love does have something to do with them all. In fact, I believe that if we've ever wanted someone's love, then we've known what competition really means.

Helen Ross was a good friend who taught teachers, doctors, and psychiatrists and consulted with professionals working with children and families all over the world. She was one of the great people of our age in the understanding of the dynamic development of human beings. After one operation for cancer and some subsequent therapy, Helen chose to refuse treatment when her cancer reappeared. One day when I visited her, I found Helen very frail, yet interested in all that I had to tell her about our television work and her Pittsburgh friends. Some of the time I just held her hand and we said nothing. We didn't have to.

After one of those silences, Helen said to me, "Do you ever pray for people, Fred?"

"Of course I do." So I said, "Dear God, encircle us with Thy love wherever we may be."

And Helen replied, "That's what it is, isn't it?—it's love. That's what it's all about."

Helen was eighty-eight when she died. She had spent most of her adult life working at understanding the complexities of human growth and development, and her summation of life was that love is what it's all about.

It's You I Like

It's you I like,
It's not the things you wear,
It's not the way you do your hair,
But it's you I like.

The way you are right now,
The way down deep inside you,
Not the things that hide you,
Not your toys, they're just beside you.

But it's you I like, every part of you,
Your skin, your eyes, your feelings
Whether old or new.

I hope that you'll remember
Even when you're feeling blue
That it's you I like,
It's you yourself, it's you,
It's you . . . I . . . like!

There's something unique about being a member of a family that really needs you in order to function well. One of the deepest longings a person can have is to feel needed and essential.

Actor David Carradine, son of John Carradine, said in gratitude of his father's accomplishments, "I could stand on his shoulders and feel twice as tall." That each generation could stand on the shoulders of the last and feel twice as tall is a poetic hope for all our families.

My own friend and companion, when I was
little and didn't yet have a sister, was Mitzi,
a brown, wire-haired mongrel. We played
and had long "conversations" during which
she heard many of my secrets and shared
my joys and sadnesses. We ran in the fields
and huddled together through thunder-
storms. I gave a great deal of myself to
Mitzi, and she faithfully reflected that self
back to me, helping me learn more about
who I was and, in those early days, what I
was feeling. When she died, she went on
teaching me—about loss and grief . . . and
about the renewal of hope and joy.

The gifts we treasure most over the years are often small and simple. In easy times and in tough times, what seems to matter most is the way we show those nearest us that we've been listening to their needs, to their joys, and to their challenges.

I received a letter from a parent who wrote: "Mister Rogers, how do you do it? I wish I were like you. I want to be patient and quiet and even-tempered, and always speak respectfully to my children. But that just isn't my personality. I often lose my patience and even scream at my children. I want to change from an impatient person into a patient person, from an angry person into a gentle one."

Just as it takes time for children to understand what real love is, it takes time for parents to understand that being *always* patient, quiet, even-tempered, and respectful isn't necessarily what "good" parents are. In fact, parents help children by expressing a wide range of feelings—including appropriate anger. All children need to see that the adults in their lives can feel anger and not hurt themselves or anyone else when they feel that way.

As parents, we need to try to find the security within ourselves to accept the fact that children and parents won't always like each other's actions, that there will be times when parents and children won't be able to be friends, and that there will be times of real anger in families. But we need to know, at the same time, that moments of conflict have nothing to do with whether parents and children really love one another. It's our continuing love for our children that makes us want them to become all they can be, capable of making sound choices.

Forgiveness is a strange thing. It can sometimes be easier to forgive our enemies than our friends. It can be hardest of all to forgive people we love. Like all of life's important coping skills, the ability to forgive and the capacity to let go of resentments most likely take root very early in our lives.

Mutually caring relationships require kindness and patience, tolerance, optimism, joy in the other's achievements, confidence in oneself, and the ability to give without undue thought of gain. We need to accept the fact that it's not in the power of any human being to provide all these things all the time. For any of us, mutually caring relationships will also always include some measure of unkindness and impatience, intolerance, pessimism, envy, self-doubt, and disappointment.

In times of stress, the best thing we can do for each other is to listen with our ears and our hearts and to be assured that our questions are just as important as our answers.

One of the strongest things we have to wrestle with in our lives is the significance of the longing for perfection in ourselves and in the people bound to us by friendship or parenthood or childhood.

The World According to Mister Rogers

The greatest gift you ever give is your honest self.

In the giving of help, a parent experiences one of the best feelings that any of us can have: that life has meaning because we are needed by someone else. Watching a baby grow with our help tells us other things we like to feel about ourselves: that we are competent and loving.

It's not always easy for a father to understand the interests and ways of his son. It seems the songs of our children may be in keys we've never tried. The melody of each generation emerges from all that's gone before. Each one of us contributes in some unique way to the composition of life.

I believe that infants and babies
whose mothers give them loving comfort
whenever and however they can are
truly the fortunate ones. I think they're
more likely to find life's times of trouble
manageable, and I think they may
also turn out to be the adults most able
to pass loving concern along to the
generations that follow after them.

Learning and loving go hand in hand. My grandfather was one of those people who loved to live and loved to teach. Every time I was with him, he'd show me something about the world or something about myself that I hadn't even thought of yet. He'd help me find something wonderful in the smallest of things, and ever so carefully, he helped me understand the enormous worth of every human being. My grandfather was not a professional teacher, but the way he treated me (the way he *loved* me) and the things he did with me, served me as well as any teacher I've ever known.

I do love being a grandfather, and I wonder if it wasn't because my grandfather McFeely loved me so much, and I had such a good time with him.

You bring all you ever were and are to any relationship you have today.

In the external scheme of things, shining moments are as brief as the twinkling of an eye, yet such twinklings are what eternity is made of—moments when we human beings can say "I love you," "I'm proud of you," "I forgive you," "I'm grateful for you." That's what eternity is made of: invisible, imperishable *good stuff*.

We need to help people to discover the true meaning of love. Love is generally confused with dependence. Those of us who have grown in true love know that we can love only in proportion to our capacity for independence.

Children who have learned to be
comfortably dependent can become not
only comfortably independent, but can also
become comfortable with having people
depend on them. They can lean, or stand
and be leaned upon, because they know
what a good feeling it can be to feel needed.

Love is like infinity: You can't have more or less infinity, and you can't compare two things to see if they're "equally infinite." Infinity just is, and that's the way I think love is, too.

Listening is a very active awareness of
the coming together of at least two lives.
Listening, as far as I'm concerned, is
certainly a prerequisite of love. One of the
most essential ways of saying "I love you" is
being a receptive listener.

Listening is where love begins: listening to ourselves and then to our neighbors.

Human relationships are primary in all of living. When the gusty winds blow and shake our lives, if we know that people care about us, we may bend with the wind . . . but we won't break.

When we love a person, we accept him or her exactly as is: the lovely with the unlovely, the strong along with the fearful, the true mixed in with the facade, and of course, the only way we can do it is by accepting ourselves that way.

The
Challenges
of Inner
Discipline

Imagining something may be the first step in making it happen, but it takes the real time and real efforts of real people to learn things, make things, turn thoughts into deeds or visions into inventions.

What makes the difference between wishing and realizing our wishes? Lots of things, of course, but the main one, I think, is whether we link our wishes to our active work. It may take months or years, but it's far more likely to happen when we care so much that we'll work as hard as we can to make it happen. And when we're working toward the realization of our wishes, some of our greatest strengths come from the encouragement of people who care about us.

Discipline is a teaching-learning kind of relationship as the similarity of the word *disciple* suggests. By helping our children learn to be self-disciplined, we are also helping them learn how to become independent of us as, sooner or later, they must. And we are helping them learn how to be loving parents to children of their own.

What Do You Do with the Mad That You Feel?

What do you do with the mad that you feel
When you feel so mad you could bite?
When the whole wide world
Seems oh, so wrong
And nothing you do seems very right?
What do you do? Do you punch a bag?
Do you pound some clay or some dough?
Do you round up friends for a game of tag?
Or see how fast you go?

It's great to be able to stop
When you've planned a thing that's wrong.
And be able to do something else instead

And think this song:
I can stop when I want to,
Can stop when I wish,
Can stop, stop, stop anytime.
And what a good feeling to feel like this,
And know that the feeling is really mine.
Know that there's something deep inside
That helps us become what we can,
For a girl can be someday a woman
And a boy can be someday a man.

How great it is when we come to know
that times of disappointment can be
followed by times of fulfillment; that sorrow
can be followed by joy; that guilt over
falling short of our ideals can be replaced
by pride in doing all that we can; and
that anger can be channeled into creative
achievements . . . and into dreams that we
can make come true!

I like to swim, but there are some days I just don't feel much like doing it—but *I do it anyway!* I know it's good for me and I promised myself I'd do it every day, and I like to keep my promises. That's one of my disciplines. And it's a good feeling after you've tried and done something well. Inside you think, "I've kept at this and I've really learned it—not by magic, but by my own work."

There are times all during life when we
need the *inner* resources to keep ourselves
busy and productive all by ourselves.

As work grows out of play, an attitude toward work grows with it—an attitude that may persist all through our workaday life. That attitude can have a lot to do with how we accept challenges, how we can cope with failures, and whether we can find the inner fulfillment that makes working, in and of itself, worthwhile.

What makes the difference between
wishing and realizing our wishes? Lots
of things, and it may take months or
years for a wish to come true, but it's far
more likely to happen when you care so
much about a wish that you'll do all
you can to make it happen.

When we can resign ourselves to the wishes that will never come true, there can be enormous energies available within us for whatever we *can* do. I know a woman who remembers the time when her wish to have children would not be realized. She remembers the struggle of the final resignation, and then she remembers the outcome of that resignation. Enormous energies were available to her, which she used in developing uniquely creative work with young parents.

A young apprentice applied to a master carpenter for a job. The older man asked him, "Do you know your trade?" "Yes, sir!" the young man replied proudly. "Have you ever made a mistake?" the older man inquired. "No, sir!" the young man answered, feeling certain he would get the job. "Then there's no way I'm going to hire you," said the master carpenter, "because when you make one, you won't know how to fix it."

One of the greatest paradoxes about omnipotence is that we need to feel it early in life, and lose it early in life, in order to achieve a healthy, realistic, yet exciting, sense of potency later on.

There is no normal life that is free of pain. It's the very wrestling with our problems that can be the impetus for our growth.

I hope you're proud of yourself for the times you've said "yes," when all it meant was extra work for you and was seemingly helpful only to somebody else.

Often out of periods of losing come the greatest strivings toward a new winning streak.

Development comes from within. Nature
does not hurry but advances slowly.

It came to me ever so slowly that the best way to know the truth was to begin trusting what my inner truth was . . . and trying to share it—not right away—only after I had worked hard at trying to understand it.

The great poet Rainer Maria Rilke wrote: "Be patient towards all that is unsolved in your heart, and learn to love the questions themselves."

When I think of solitude, I think of an anecdote from *With the Door Open: My Experience* by the late Danish religious philosopher Johannes Anker Larsen: "The most comprehensive formula for human culture which I know was given by the old peasant who, on his death bed, obtained from his son this one promise: to sit every day for half an hour *alone* in the best room."

The World According to Mister Rogers

When I was young (about eight or ten years old), I was trying to learn so many things all at once, things like the piano and organ and algebra and cooking and typing, and I even started to take clarinet lessons. But I just didn't practice the clarinet, so I didn't learn. I think I wanted to learn by magic. I think that I had the idea that if I *got* the clarinet I would somehow know how to play it. But magic doesn't work with learning, not with anything really worthwhile.

You've Got to Do It

You can make believe it happens,
Or pretend that something's true.
You can wish or hope or contemplate
A thing you'd like to do.
But until you start to do it,
You will never see it through
'Cause the make-believe pretending
Just won't do it for you.

You've got to do it. Every little bit,
You've got to do it, do it, do it.
And when you're through,
You can know who did it,
For you did it, you did it, you did it.

It's not easy to keep trying,
But it's one good way to grow.
It's not easy to keep learning,
But I know that this is so:
When you've tried and learned,
You're bigger than you were a day ago.
It's not easy to keep trying,
But it's one way to grow.

When I was in college, I went to New York to talk to a songwriter I admired very much. I took him four or five songs that I had written and I thought he'd introduce me to Tin Pan Alley and it would be the beginning of my career. After I played him my songs, he said, "You have very nice songs. Come back when you have a barrelful."

A barrelful of songs! That would mean hundreds of songs. I can still remember the disappointment I felt as I traveled all the way back to college. Nevertheless, that man's counsel was more inspired than I realized. It took me years to understand that. But, of course, what he knew was that if I *really* wanted to be a songwriter, I'd have to write songs, not just think about the five I *had* written. And so, after the initial disappointment, I got to work; and through the years, one by one, I *have* written a barrelful.

In fact, the barrel's overflowing now, and I can tell you, the more I wrote, the better the songs became, and the more those songs expressed what was real within me.

To me, what makes someone successful is managing a healthy combination of wishing and doing. Wishing doesn't make anything happen, but it certainly can be the start of some important happenings. I hope you'll feel good enough about yourself, your yesterdays and your today, that you'll continue to wish and dream all you can. And that you'll do all you can to help the best of your wishes come true.

I'm proud of you for all the wishing and doing that has helped you get to this point in your lives, and I hope you are, too.

There's an old Italian proverb: *Qui va piano, va sano, va lentano.* That means: "The person who goes quietly, goes with health and goes far." Hurrying up and using a lot of shortcuts doesn't get us very far at all.

One summer, midway through Seminary, I was on a weekend vacation in a little town in New England. I decided on Sunday to go hear a visiting preacher in the little town's chapel. I heard the worst sermon I could have ever imagined. I sat in the pew thinking, "He's going against every rule they're teaching us about preaching. What a waste of time!" That's what I thought until the very end of the sermon when I happened to see the person beside me with tears in her eyes whispering, "He said exactly what I needed to hear." It was then that I knew something very important had happened in that service. The woman beside me had come in need. Somehow the words of that poorly crafted sermon had been translated into a message that spoke to her heart. On the other hand, I had come in judgment, and I heard nothing but the faults.

It was a long time before I realized it, but that sermon's effect on the person beside me turned out to be one of the great lessons of my life. Thanks to that preacher and listener-in-need, I now know that the space between a person doing his or her best to deliver a message of good news and the needy listener is holy ground. Recognizing that seems to have allowed me to forgive myself for being the accuser that day. In fact, that New England Sunday experience has fueled my desire to be a better advocate, a better "neighbor," wherever I am.

I wrote in a song that in the long, long trip of growing, there are stops along the way. It's important to know when we need to stop, reflect, and receive. In our competitive world, that might be called a waste of time. I've learned that those times can be the preamble to periods of enormous growth. Recently, I declared a day to be alone with myself. I took a long drive and played a tape. When I got to the mountains, I read and prayed and listened and slept. In fact, I can't remember having a calmer sleep in a long, long time. The next day I went back to work and did more than I usually get done in three days.

No matter how old we are, we need to know that the people who are important to us really do care about us. But feeling good about who we are doesn't come just from people telling us they like us. It comes from inside of us: knowing when we've done something helpful or when we've worked hard to learn something difficult or when we've "stopped" just when we were about to do something we shouldn't, or when we've been especially kind to someone else. Along with the times we're feeling good about who we are, we can experience times when we're feeling bad about who we are. That's just a part of being human.

It's true that we take a great deal of our own upbringing on into our adult lives and our lives as parents; but it's true, too, that we can change some of the things that we would like to change. It can be hard, but it can be done.

We

Are

All

Neighbors

It's no secret that I like to get to know people—and not just the outside stuff of their lives. I like to try to understand the meaning of who people are and what they're saying to me.

All of us, at some time or other, need help. Whether we're giving or receiving help, each one of us has something valuable to bring to this world. That's one of the things that connects us as neighbors—in our own way, each one of us is a giver and a receiver.

As human beings, our job in life is to help people realize how rare and valuable each one of us really is, that each of us has something that no one else has—or ever will have—something inside that is unique to all time. It's our job to encourage each other to discover that uniqueness and to provide ways of developing its expression.

I've had lots of heroes—lots of people I've wanted to be like. To this day, I can still feel the excitement in 1944 as I opened the first installment of my Charles Atlas exercise course. I had saved my money ($19.00) and had sent away for those lessons that I thought would help me look like Atlas himself holding up the world. In 1944, I was a chubby and weak sixteen-year-old, and Charles Atlas was trim and strong. I did the exercises every morning—some of them even had me hanging on a bar at a doorjamb. Many months and many lessons later, I still

The World According to Mister Rogers

didn't look like Charles Atlas. Now, happily, I don't need to.

Maybe it's natural, especially when we're little and feel weak, to choose "outside" kinds of heroes and superheroes who can keep us safe in a scary world.

My next hero was a "big man on campus" in our high school: Jim Stumbaugh. He could do anything. A letterman in basketball, football, and track, he made all A's. Both of his parents were teachers, but his dad died during our freshman year. Who knows? Maybe that made Jim sensitive to the needs of a shy kid like me. At any rate, we beat the odds and became lifelong friends. Many years after high school when Jim's teenage son was killed in an automobile accident, I was there for him. The way he lived through that terrible time and the way he lived through his own years of cancer confirmed my pick of a hero. Jim started out looking like Charles Atlas, ended up looking like Mahatma Gandhi. What's amazing to me is that he always acted like that peace-filled Gandhi.

Yes, Gandhi's one of my heroes . . . Gandhi and Albert Schweitzer and Jane Addams (that tireless advocate of internationalism and world peace), and Bo Lozoff (who helps inmates use their time well in prison). Other heroes are Yo-Yo Ma and everyone else in the public eye who cares about beauty and refuses to bow to fast and loud sensationalism and greed. Recently I've added an "unknown hero" to my list: the person who drives the car I saw the other day, the parked car with the flashing lights and the sign that reads, "Vintage Volunteer . . . Home Delivered Meals."

So those are some of my heroes now: the Charles Atlases of my elder years! They're the kind of people who help all of us come to realize that "biggest" doesn't necessarily mean "best," that the most important things of life are *inside* things like feelings and wonder and love—and that the ultimate happiness is being able sometimes, somehow to help our neighbor become a hero too.

I have always wanted to have a neighbor
Just like you!
I've always wanted to live in a
Neighborhood with you.
So let's make the most of this beautiful day;
Since we're together we might as well say,
Would you be mine?
Could you be mine?
Won't you be my neighbor?

The older I get, the more I seem to be able to appreciate my "neighbor" (whomever I happen to be with at the moment). Oh, sure, I've always tried to love my neighbor as myself; however, the more experiences I've had, the more chances I've had to see the uniqueness of each person . . . as well as each tree, and plant, and shell, and cloud . . . the more I find myself delighting every day in the lavish gifts of God, whom I've come to believe is the greatest appreciator of all.

A high school student wrote to ask, "What was the greatest event in American history?" I can't say. However, I suspect that like so many "great" events, it was something very simple and very quiet with little or no fanfare (such as someone forgiving someone else for a deep hurt that eventually changed the course of history). The *really* important "great" things are never center stage of life's dramas; they're always "in the wings." That's why it's so essential for us to be mindful of the humble and the deep rather than the flashy and the superficial.

When I was very young, most of my childhood heroes wore capes, flew through the air, or picked up buildings with one arm. They were spectacular and got a lot of attention. But as I grew, my heroes changed, so that now I can honestly say that anyone who does anything to help a child is a hero to me.

We want to raise our children so that they can take a sense of pleasure in both their own heritage and the diversity of others.

When you combine your own intuition
with a sensitivity to other people's feelings
and moods, you may be close to the origins
of valuable human attributes such as
generosity, altruism, compassion, sympathy,
and empathy.

When I was a boy, one of my closest neighbors was Mama Bell Frampton. She was my grandmother's age, and she loved children. She not only had a front porch, she had a back porch that led right to her kitchen. Every time I needed a treat, I'd knock on her back door and she'd welcome me. "Come for toast sticks, Freddy?" She knew me well.

I would have been about five or six when Mama Bell asked if I would like her to show me how to make my own toast sticks. Well, that was quite a day. She let me put the bread in the toaster and the butter and jam on the toast, and she even let me (ever so carefully) cut the toast into four long "sticks." Seems like a simple thing, but sixty-five years later, I can still feel it—that neighbor's trust and my own pride at having made those first ones on my own. When I hear "Love your neighbor as yourself," I often think of Mama Bell because I think she really did love me. She just somehow sensed what I needed in order to grow.

A few years ago I was asked to be part of a White House meeting about children and television. Many broadcasters from all over the country were there. During my speech, I asked the audience to spend one minute thinking of someone who'd made a difference in the person they'd become. As I was leaving that enormous room, I heard something from one of the military guards who was all dressed up in white and gold, looking like a statue. I heard him whisper, "Thanks, Mister Rogers."

So I went over to him and noticed his eyes were moist, and he said, "Well, sir, as I listened to you today, I started to remember my grandfather's brother. I haven't thought about him in years. I was only seven when he died, but just before that, he gave me his favorite fishing rod. I've just been thinking, maybe that's why I like fishing so much and why I like to show the kids in my neighborhood all about it."

Well, as far as I'm concerned, the major reason for my going to Washington that day was that military guard and nourishing the memory of his great-uncle. What marvelous mysteries we're privileged to be part of! Why would that young man be assigned to guard that particular room on that particular day? Slender threads like that weave this complex fabric of our life together.

Erik Erikson, a psychologist whose insight into human development has been an important foundation of our work here in the *Neighborhood*, said that "tradition is to human beings what instinct is to animals." Imagine the chaos if animals lost their instincts. So would it be if human beings were to lose all their traditions. The study of history helps keep traditions alive. When we study how our ancestors dealt with challenges, we can (hopefully) learn from their successes and failures, and fashion our responses to challenges in even more naturally human ways.

Jane Addams, writing about her *Twenty Years at Hull House*, said, "People did not want to hear about simple things. They wanted to hear about great things—simply told."

Music has given me a way of expressing my feelings and my thoughts, and it has also given me a way of understanding more about life. For example, as you play together in a symphony orchestra, you can appreciate that each musician has something fine to offer. Each one is different, though, and you each have a different "song to sing." When you sing together, you make one voice. That's true of all endeavors, not just musical ones. Finding ways to harmonize our uniqueness with the uniqueness of others can be the most fun—and the most rewarding—of all.

In every neighborhood, all across our country, there are good people insisting on a good start for the young, and doing something about it.

Fred Rogers' Acceptance Speech
Television Hall of Fame
February, 1999

Fame is a four-letter word; and like *tape* or *zoom* or *face* or *pain* or *life* or *love,* what ultimately matters is what we do with it.

I feel that those of us in television are chosen to be servants. It doesn't matter what our particular job, we are chosen to help meet the deeper needs of those who watch and listen—day and night!

The conductor of the orchestra at the Hollywood Bowl grew up in a family that had little interest in music, but he often tells people he found his early inspiration from the fine musicians on television.

Last month a thirteen-year-old boy abducted an eight-year-old girl; and when people asked him why, he said he learned about it on TV. "Something different to try," he said. "Life's cheap; what does it matter?"

Well, life *isn't* cheap. It's the greatest mystery of any millennium, and television needs to do all it can to broadcast that . . . to show and tell what the good in life is all about.

But how do we make goodness attractive? By doing whatever we can do to bring courage to those whose lives move near our own—by treating our "neighbor" at least as well as we treat ourselves and allowing *that* to inform everything that we produce.

Who in your life has been such a servant

to you . . . who has helped you love the good that grows within you? Let's just take ten seconds to think of some of those people who have loved us and wanted what was best for us in life—those who have encouraged us to become who we are tonight—just ten seconds of silence.

No matter where they are—either here or in heaven—imagine how pleased those people must be to know that you thought of them right now.

We all have only one life to live on earth. And through television, we have the choice of encouraging others to demean this life or to cherish it in creative, imaginative ways.

On behalf of all of us at Family Communications and the Public Broadcasting Service, I thank you for all the good that you do in this unique enterprise . . . and for wanting our *Neighborhood* to be part of this celebration tonight. Thank you very much.

If you could only sense how important you are to the lives of those you meet; how important you can be to the people you may never even dream of. There is something of yourself that you leave at every meeting with another person.

I often think of what Will Durant wrote in *The Story of Civilization:* "Civilization is a stream with banks. The stream is sometimes filled with blood from people killing, stealing, shouting, and doing things historians usually record—while, on the banks, unnoticed, people build homes, make love, raise children, sing songs, write poetry, whittle statues. The story of civilization is the story of what happens on the banks."

Whether we're a preschooler or a young teen, a graduating college senior or a retired person, we human beings all want to know that we're acceptable, that our being alive somehow makes a difference in the lives of others.

The more I think about it, the more I wonder if *God* and *neighbor* are somehow One. "Loving God, Loving neighbor"—the same thing? For me, coming to recognize that God loves *every* neighbor is the ultimate appreciation!

The real issue in life is not how many blessings we have, but what we do with our blessings. Some people have many blessings and hoard them. Some have few and give everything away.

I don't know that I'll be alive when my grandsons have children, and so they just may be the last Rogerses that I'm acquainted with on this earth. I know they will have lots inside of them to give to their children or nieces or nephews. But still, it is really fun for me to see them doing things that I know Rogerses have done for a long, long time. There is a continuity that goes through the generations. My friend and teacher, Dr. Margaret McFarland, used to say, "I love being part of the beach of life— I like being one of the grains of sand."

I have always called talking about feelings "important talk." Knowing that our feelings are natural and normal for all of us can make it easier for us to share them with one another.

The purpose of life is to listen—to yourself, to your neighbor, to your world and to God and, when the time comes, to respond in as helpful a way as you can find . . . from within and without.

Please think of the children *first*. If you ever have anything to do with their entertainment, their food, their toys, their custody, their day or night care, their health care, their education—listen to the children, learn about them, learn from them. *Think of the children first.*

One of the greatest dignities of humankind
is that each successive generation is invested
in the welfare of each new generation.

I think the young feel pressured by the older generation. But I realized it isn't just the older generation doing the pressuring. Young people are pressuring older people to change, too, and it can make us feel uncomfortable. But it isn't all bad either. I know how much I learned from my parents and teachers, and now I know for sure that I'm learning from my children and the young people I work with. I don't do everything they want me to do, and they don't do everything I want them to do, but we know down deep we'd really be impoverished if we didn't have each other.

More and more I've come to understand that *listening* is one of the most important things we can do for one another. Whether the other be an adult or a child, our engagement in listening to who that person is can often be our greatest gift. Whether that person is speaking or playing or dancing, building or singing or painting, if we care, we can listen.

From a Public Service Announcement
Following the Events of September 11, 2001

If you grew up with our *Neighborhood*, you may remember how we sometimes talked about difficult things. There were days . . . even beautiful days . . . that weren't happy. In fact, there were some that were really sad.

Well, we've had a lot of days like that in our whole world. We've seen what some people do when they don't know anything else to do with their anger.

I'm convinced that when we help our children find healthy ways of dealing with their feelings—ways that don't hurt them or anyone else—we're helping to make our world a safer, better place.

The World According to Mister Rogers

I would like to tell you what I often told you when you were much younger: *I like you just the way you are.*

And what's more, I'm so grateful to you for helping the children in your life to know that you'll do everything you can to keep them safe and to help them express their feelings in ways that will bring healing in many different neighborhoods.

It's very dramatic when two people come together to work something out. It's easy to take a gun and annihilate your opposition, but what is really exciting to me is to see people with differing views come together and finally respect each other.

The world needs a sense of worth, and it will achieve it only by its people feeling that they are worthwhile.

There's the good guy and the bad guy in all of us, but knowing that doesn't ever need to overwhelm us. Whatever we adults can do to help ourselves—and anybody else—discover that that's true can really make a difference in this life.

Peace means far more than the opposite
of war!

I have long believed that the way to know a spiritual sense is to know it in our real life. I think the best way to understand about God and peace is to know about peace in our everyday lives.

The World According to Mister Rogers

Beside my chair is a saying in French. It inspires me every day. It's a sentence from Saint-Exupéry's *The Little Prince,* and it reads, *"L'essential est invisible pour les yeux."* (What is essential is invisible to the eyes.) The closer we get to know the truth of that sentence, the closer I feel we get to wisdom.

That which has real value in life in any millennium is very simple. Very deep and very simple! It happens inside of us—in the "essential invisible" part of us, and that is what allows everyone to be a potential neighbor.

What matters isn't how a person's inner life finally puts together the alphabet and numbers of his outer life. What really matters is whether he uses the alphabet for the declaration of a war or the description of a sunrise—his numbers for the final count at Buchenwald or the specifics of a brand-new bridge.

I find out more and more every day how important it is for people to share their memories.

The urge to make and build seems to be an almost universal human characteristic. It goes way beyond meeting our need for survival and seems to be the expression of some deep-rooted part of being human. It isn't surprising then that these acts of creation should be such a large part of children's play. But we don't have to understand all of someone else's creative efforts. What's important is that we communicate our respect for their attempts to express what's inside themselves.

Play does seem to open up another part
of the mind that is always there, but that,
since childhood, may have become closed
off and hard to reach. When we treat
children's play as seriously as it deserves,
we are helping them feel the joy that's
to be found in the creative spirit. We're
helping ourselves stay in touch with that
spirit, too. It's the things we play with
and the people who help us play that make
a great difference in our lives.

As different as we are from one another,
as unique as each one of us is, we are much
more the same than we are different.
That may be the most essential message
of all, as we help our children grow
toward being caring, compassionate, and
charitable adults.

Imagine what our real neighborhoods would be like if each of us offered, as a matter of course, just one kind word to another person. There have been so many stories about the lack of courtesy, the impatience of today's world, road rage and even restaurant rage. Sometimes, all it takes is one kind word to nourish another person. Think of the ripple effect that can be created when we nourish someone. One kind empathetic word has a wonderful way of turning into many.

One of the mysteries is that as unlike as we are, one human being from another, we also share much in common. Our lives begin the same way, by birth. The love and interdependence of parents and children is universal, and so are the many difficulties parents and children have in becoming separate from one another. As we grow, we laugh and cry at many of the same things, and fear many of the same things. At the end, we all leave the same way—by death. Yet no two threads—no two lives—in that vast tapestry of existence have ever been, or ever will be, the same.

The World According to Mister Rogers

When I was a boy and I would see scary things in the news, my mother would say to me, "Look for the helpers. You will always find people who are helping." To this day, especially in times of "disaster," I remember my mother's words, and I am always comforted by realizing that there are still so many helpers—so many caring people in this world.

When I was ordained, it was for a special ministry, that of serving children and families through television. I consider that what I do through *Mister Rogers' Neighborhood* is my ministry. A ministry doesn't have to be only through a church, or even through an ordination. And I think we all can minister to others in this world by being compassionate and caring. I hope you will feel good enough about yourselves that you will want to minister to others, and that you will find your own unique ways to do that.

You don't ever have to do anything sensational for people to love you. When I say, "It's you I like," I'm talking about that part of you that knows that life is far more than anything you can ever see or hear or touch . . . that deep part of you that allows you to stand for those things without which humankind cannot survive: *love* that conquers hate, *peace* that rises triumphant over war, and *justice* that proves more powerful than greed.

So in all that you do in all of your life, I wish you the strength and the grace to make those choices which will allow you and your neighbor to become the best of whoever you are.

ACKNOWLEDGMENTS

Each one of us at Family Communications, Inc. has been privileged and blessed to have had the incredible gift of a relationship with Fred Rogers, most of us for decades. Over the years we've worked with him, we've laughed with him, struggled with him, and strived with him, shared our interests and concerns and feelings with him, and loved him. He helped us find the courage to be ourselves, and we've all grown professionally and personally because of what he's given us.

After Fred Rogers' death, Bob Miller at Hyperion Books, a friend for twenty years, suggested that we compile a collection of quotations so that people could continue to share in and learn from Fred Rogers' wisdom. We've been especially fortunate to have Mary Ellen O'Neill as our editor because of the sensitivity and genuine care that she's given to this work. Her assistant, Elisa Lee, was a great help in organizing and collating the material.

Our thanks go to the whole FCI team, all of whom have been a great support, directly or indirectly. Particular thanks go to Bill Isler, who as president of FCI oversaw this project from its beginning to its fruition with his caring leadership and deep respect for Fred and Joanne Rogers and the Rogers family. Special thanks to Hedda Bluestone Sharapan and Cathy Cohen Droz, who gave their thoughtful and careful attention to the quotations as well as to the organization and layout of the manuscript. We're also deeply grateful to the Rogers family for their support of our continuing work at FCI.

Fred Rogers dedicated his life and his work to serving children and families through television and beyond. Under his guidance over the years, we at FCI have developed a wide variety of materials—all supporting relationships between children and their families and between children and the childcare providers and other professionals who care for them. Since Fred Rogers' death, many people have asked us,

"What's next?" just as people often asked Fred, "What's next?" His answer was always, "*This* is next." And so is ours. *Mister Rogers' Neighborhood* continues to be broadcast on PBS, and we're building on the work that Fred Rogers began, taking his philosophy and approach into new arenas. We remain a strong company, and we're proud to carry on his legacy.

BIOGRAPHY OF FRED ROGERS

Fred McFeely Rogers was best known as "Mister Rogers," creator, host, writer, composer, and puppeteer for the longest-running program on PBS, *Mister Rogers' Neighborhood*.

His journey to the *Neighborhood* began in 1951 during his senior year at Rollins College, when he became intrigued by the educational potential of television. After graduating with a degree in music composition from Rollins, he joined NBC in New York as an assistant producer for *The Kate Smith Hour*, *The Voice of Firestone*, and the *NBC Opera Theatre*. In 1952, he married Joanne Byrd, a pianist and fellow Rollins graduate.

Returning to his hometown area of western Pennsylvania in 1953, he helped found Pittsburgh's public television station, WQED, and co-produced an hour-long live daily children's program, *The Children's Corner*, for which he also worked behind the scenes as puppeteer and musician. To broaden his understanding of children, Fred Rogers began his lifelong study of children and families at the Graduate School of Child Development in the University of Pittsburgh School of Medicine. There he had the opportunity to work closely with young children under the supervision of Dr. Margaret B. McFarland, clinical psychologist. He also completed a Master of Divinity degree at the Pittsburgh Theological Seminary and was ordained as a Presbyterian minister in 1963 with the unique charge of serving children and families through the media.

Fred Rogers has been the recipient of virtually every major award in television and education. He has received honorary degrees from more than forty colleges and universities, and in 2002 was awarded the Presidential Medal of Freedom, the nation's highest civilian honor.

In 1971, Fred Rogers founded Family Communications, Inc. (FCI), a non-profit company for the production of *Mister Rogers' Neighborhood* and other materials. Building on its beginnings in broadcast television production, FCI has expanded into almost all forms of media—print, audio, video, training workshops, the Internet, DVD, and traveling exhibits. For information about Family Communications, visit the website (www.fci.org).

The company's ongoing work continues to be guided by Fred Rogers' mission of communicating with young children and their families in clear, honest, nurturing, and supportive ways.